MALCOLM FOR PRESIDENT

MALCOLM FOR PRESIDENT

By Tom Mason & Dan Danko

SCHOLASTIC INC.
New York   Toronto   London   Auckland   Sydney
Mexico City   New Delhi   Hong Kong

I was a normal kid once.

No way! I was _never_ normal. But at least I could fake it. Until those test scores came in and I got moved to the Krelboyne class. The "special class" of math whizzes and spastic dancers — prime targets for rejection, humiliation, and school bullies.

Every morning, after I've pushed my older brother, Reese, and my little brother, Dewey, out of the way, I look at myself in the bathroom mirror.

Do I see a genius? Hardly. Do I see a supernerd? I hope not.

I see me. A kid in the middle of four brothers, a mom, and a dad. I know what the test scores and school counselors said, but I don't feel any different.

I mean, I like video games. Like the kind where you can blast stuff into digital bits. I like any day when there's no school. Not just Saturdays and

Sundays, but days when Presidents were born and days when I fake a stomachache. And I like it when my brother Reese leaves me alone.

Come to think of it, I like it when pretty much everyone leaves me alone. That's probably not going to happen anytime soon, though. Maybe the day after I move to the moon.

CHAPTER ONE

Reese started it.

He bet me his dessert that I couldn't name all the U.S. Presidents in reverse order, starting from right now and working back to number one, George Washington. Like Reese would know if I was right or wrong.

Friday night, Dewey, Reese, and I were having an early dinner. Dad was working late, and Mom actually wanted to *watch* something on TV. So she turned us loose in the kitchen with microwaved food and some salad.

As soon as Mom left the kitchen, Reese made the bet.

"You can't do it," he dared.

"Of course I can," I countered. "It's easy."

"As easy as, say, your dessert?" he tempted.

"Bush, Clinton, Bush, Reagan, Carter, Ford, Nixon," I started. I got all the way down to number twenty-three, Benjamin Harrison, before the trouble started.

"Ow!" Something hot hit my forehead. It was long. It was round. It was a spaghetti noodle. I looked up. "Ow!" Again! This time, Reese flicked a meatball at me. It bounced off my nose and into Dewey's mouth.

"Thanks, Reese," Dewey squeaked with his mouth full. "Do it again." He waited for more meatball treasures.

Reese flicked another one at me. This one went sailing past my head and bounced off the kitchen clock.

Reese tries hard, but he can't aim. With a casual flick of my index finger, I shot two croutons back at him. One lodged in his nose. Bull's-eye!

By the time he sneezed it out, I was at the freezer. I grabbed the frozen waffles and ducked. A spoonful of bacon bits smothered in lo-cal salad dressing flew past my head. It left a butterfly-shaped splat on the stove. I laughed — then, I felt something cold on my back. *Really* cold. And wet.

"Aww, Dewey!" I cried.

"Gotcha!" he giggled.

My little brother is small and quiet in an easy-to-forget-he's-there way. His innocent face makes him a perfect, silent sneak.

A sneak who just then had climbed up on the counter and dumped a container of spaghetti sauce down the back of my shirt. He took Reese's side? How fair is that? Whatever happened to one against one against one?

This . . . means . . . war!

I grabbed a jar of pickles and a bowl of leftover baked beans. Reese grabbed the mayo, a spoon, and a box of twenty-four frozen mini-egg rolls. Wish I'd seen those first!

Splat! My chest exploded in cholesterol. Dewey had a carton of eggs. He hurled a second one my way. I ducked and it hit Reese in his ear.

That's cool. Reese retaliated with a barrage of frozen egg rolls that totally missed Dewey. They ricocheted off the sinkful of dirty dishes. And the stove. And the coffeepot.

With his second batch of egg rolls, Reese was ready for more action. Dewey held an egg in each of his tiny hands.

This called for drastic steps. I had to take them both out with one mega-toss. I scooped up a handful of the beans and hurled them shotgun-style. They flew across the kitchen in a beautiful baked brown arc.

You couldn't paint a prettier picture. I licked my fingers and watched the beans hit their targets: Reese's face, Dewey's open mouth, the kitchen clock, the toaster, the walls, and . . .

Mom's hair?

Underneath? Mom's *very* unhappy face.

We froze, waiting for the explosion of Mom-rage that we knew was coming. On the yell scale of 1 to 10, this looked like it could go all the way to 20, maybe 25.

But she didn't explode. She didn't send us to bed. Or make us sit facing the wall for two hours. Instead she shoved us out to the backyard.

"You like playing with your food?" she shouted. "Then play your hearts out!"

Mom supplied us with more cool ammunition: frozen drumsticks, squirt cheese, waffles, syrup, applesauce, and tons of other stuff from the fridge.

"You boys play nice," she said. "And when I get back from the mall, you better *still* be playing."

"Where's she going?" Reese asked, his face covered in corn pudding. His shirtsleeves oozed mashed potatoes.

I peeked out from behind a tree. I cocked my arm and let fly a drumstick, smacking Dewey in his butt.

"I don't know," I answered. "I hope she's getting dessert!"

CHAPTER TWO

"**T**he Electoral College is actually a misnomer," Dabney said to the rest of the class. "It's not really a school."

No, the Electoral College isn't a school. But *this* one is, and I'm stuck in it. We're doing government today because class elections are coming up. That means the hallways are wallpapered with banners. Student candidates who take this way too seriously are already making speeches. Everyone will cast a vote. And nothing will ever change.

But my fellow Krelboynes are loving every brain-numbing minute of it.

The Krelboynes are a "gifted class." Translation? Social misfits. They do math without a calculator, get their homework done weeks ahead of the due date, and actually look *forward* to the annual science fair.

I'm one of them. But I try not to admit it too often. It's like having a "KICK ME!" sign permanently taped to your back.

I think politics is way boring — like the Golf Channel or cleaning my room or one of my dad's stories.

But not the Krelboynes. In today's class discussion of government, they were neck-deep.

"It's . . . called . . . checks . . . and . . . balances," my friend Stevie Kenarban wheezed in the time it takes to get a pizza delivered.

"And what's our system of government called?" the teacher asked.

"The two-party system," Dabney yelled out with a little too much enthusiasm.

"And the two parties?" she followed up.

"Democrats and Republicans," Eraserhead offered.

"Very good, class." The teacher kept talking. Asking questions, taking answers from the overeager Krelboynes, and nodding with happiness at their always-correct answers.

And me? I'm doing my best to keep my eyes open. I thought about my favorite television shows. I listed my favorite baseball players in alphabetical order. I broke down the process of oxidation and its effect on a bicycle left out in the rain.

Suddenly, it totally dawns on me. All this talk of elections, Presidents, and government rings a bell. Presidents' Day + holiday − school = day off!

That's the great thing about Presidents and other ancient dead guys: They're always having birthdays and junk like that. Thanks to one of them, this weekend is a total three-day holiday. And for the bonus round: Francis is coming home!

Francis is my older brother. My *cooler*, surf-god–looking brother. Picture a blond version of the coolest guy you know, riding a tasty wave and getting mobbed by cute girls. What he's doing in my family, I don't know. But I'm grateful.

Francis is away at military school learning right from wrong and other not-so-fun stuff. But a three-day weekend means he gets to come home for a visit. That is so awesome! Nothing could ruin my day now . . .

"We nominate Malcolm!" Eraserhead shouted out. The whole classroom erupted in cheers and applause.

Nominate me? Nominate me for *what*?

CHAPTER THREE

"**M**alcolm! Malcolm! Malcolm!" my classmates chanted.

Malcolm what? I had turned in my homework. I'd read all those boring chapters in the book. Krelboynes have already destroyed my social life. What *else* could they want?

"Stevie," I whispered. "Did I miss something?"

"The . . . class . . . elections," he explained. "We . . . just . . . nominated . . . you to run . . . for President . . . of our . . . grade!"

"Class President?!" I exploded. "Is everyone crazy?" Class President? I don't even want to be *in* class. Well, not as a Krelboyne, anyway.

"Very good, class," the teacher said. "The best way to learn about government is to experience it firsthand, with your own candidate."

Krelboyne fingers pointed at me.

You know that feeling you feel, like, when you're in a dream? Stuff is happening all around you, but none of it feels real? It was like that.

Under the teacher's direction, the Krelboynes formed the Krelboyne Independent Party. For the upcoming student elections, they've selected me to be their nominee for President.

Okay, maybe *some* people would like that. But not me! It's the *last* thing I want. It wouldn't be so bad if it got me out of class, but being Class President is like volunteering for extra homework. There are after-school meetings, early-morning meetings, meetings on Saturdays, and all kinds of stuff to read. And what do you get in return? I don't know, but it can't be worth all that extra work. At least it's only President for my grade, and not for the whole school.

Biggest lesson learned today? It's important to pay attention in class. It has nothing to do with learning or getting into a good college. You have to pay attention so you don't get volunteered for things you would never ever in a million years volunteer for.

"Malcolm, you're the man!" Flora said.

"Malcolm for President!" Eraserhead shouted.

"It's time . . . for a change . . . and that . . . change is . . . Malcolm!" You can guess who said that.

"Krelboyne Independent Party! Oh, yes!" After he said that, Lloyd started doing a little dance best described as "not-a-dance."

Finally, the bell rang for lunch. I ran to the cafeteria. Otherwise, I might get nominated for something else.

I was almost looking forward to Mom's usual "I-think-this-baloney's-still-good" sandwich and some Chex Party Mix with all the good pieces gone.

Unfortunately, lunch turned out to be the first official meeting of the nominee (me) and the Krelboyne Independent Party Advisory Committee, or KIPAC.

I decided to start off the meeting with a simple statement of my goals. "I don't want to be your candidate."

"Look, Malcolm, peer identification carries a lot of weight in an election," Dabney explained. "You're the most normal-looking of all the Krelboynes."

Okay, so that's probably a compliment. Me, the most normal Krelboyne. But then I heard Reese's voice echoing in my head: "Dude, that's like being the prettiest bug under my shoe."

"It's a thin line between genius and *evil* genius," Eraserhead offered. "It runs in your family. We've heard legendary tales of Francis."

Well, who hadn't? He *was* a legend here. Before he got caught, of course.

"You have the genetic makeup of your brother Reese," Flora said.

Ouch. That *totally* stung!

Then they started tossing campaign issues around. They had the lamest ideas.

"No more book reports," Eraserhead said.

"That's not gonna fly," I explained. "Teachers and book reports go together like chocolate and peanut butter."

"I'd ... like ... my own ... parking ... space," Stevie said.

"But you don't drive," I reminded him.

"I will . . . some day," he defended.

"Fewer A's. More A+'s," Lloyd said. "My mom's got a birthday next month."

Ideas flew faster than I could count.

"More extra credit."

"More allergy days."

"Expanded . . . Internet . . . access."

"No more braces."

I just looked at the kid who said that. He wasn't a Krelboyne, and I'd never seen him before. He had a mouth filled with those hideous metal tracks that twisted and bent his teeth like something from a movie I'm not supposed to see until I'm seventeen.

"I just don't like braces," he explained. "If you want my vote, you've got to appeal to *my* special interest." He walked away.

The Krelboynes resumed their list of campaign issues, but I'd had enough. I was about to stand up and totally withdraw from the election, get my name off the ballot, and forget this whole nightmare ever existed.

Until Stevie wheeled over to me and held out his hand.

"I want . . . to be . . . your . . . campaign . . . manager," he gasped.

I looked at him as if he'd fallen from Mars. He was beaming, hoping that I'd accept. With his giant, thick glasses he looked more like an owl than ever before.

How could I refuse a friend? "Okay," I acknowledged as I shook his hand. If Stevie thinks the election is important enough to want to be on my team, then I'll run for this dopey office.

"I want . . . to stand . . . next to . . . greatness," he said. "To make . . . a difference." He paused. "And maybe . . . meet some . . . girls."

"Oh, yeah," I said sarcastically. "Girls really go for the Class President from the Krelboyne Independent Party."

"And . . . his . . . campaign . . . manager."

So there it is. I'm the man. I'm the nominee for Class President from the All-Nerd Party.

You know what kind of people get involved in school politics? The kind who can't play sports 'cause they'll get dirty. They're the ones whose parents actually drive them to school in cars that always look showroom-clean and cost as much as a house.

They're the ones who really believe they can change the cafeteria menu from Salisbury steak to meatless all-soy loaf. The kind of people who volunteer to work in the office during their free period.

They're the bossy, confident, perfect-teeth kids with dry-cleaned clothes and belts that match their shoes.

I'm wearing Reese's hand-me-down shirt, Francis's old belt, and – even

though this might be too much infor-
mation — yesterday's underwear.

Class President? Why couldn't I be
nominated for President of the Cold
Pizza for Breakfast Club or the Video
Games Forever Society? Something
that makes sense.

Well, maybe it'll be okay. After all,
somebody's got to lose the election,
and maybe it'll be me. That would be
sweet.

CHAPTER FOUR

"One, two, three, shove!"

"Use your muscles! All of them!"

The next day, that was the first thing I heard at school. And it wasn't the voices in my head. I only wished it was. The Milson twins were pushing their oversized bodies against the Krelboyne trailer, trying to move it off the bricks that held it in place.

"I felt it budge a little," Mike Milson said, stretching out his enormous arm.

"Trailers can't take the heat," his brother Ike noted.

They stopped when they saw me.

"Hello, Malcolm," Mike sneered. "We hear you're running for Class President."

"Yeah. President," Ike repeated.

I shrugged. I couldn't really deny it, since there was a "MALCOLM FOR PRESIDENT" sign hanging over the trailer door. Not that they could read it.

"We're *also* running for Class President." Mike looked at Ike. "And Vice President."

"We formed the anti-Krelboyne party," Ike smirked.

Okay, that's going too far! I mean, Krelboynes are weird and stuff, but there's no reason to do that.

The line on the Milson twins? Not very bright, but

very strong. Potentially, they could intimidate voters. The only good thing about them is that by tomorrow they'll have forgotten about the Krelboynes and formed the "Athletes Against Broccoli" party.

"Look out!" Ike came running at me. I jumped out of the way and he crashed into the trailer. "With enough votes," he grunted, "we're gonna push the Krelboynes into the next state!"

"Well, good luck," I said as I slowly backed away.

"Hey, thanks!" Mike offered cheerfully. "Vote for the Milsons, okay?"

"Whatever," I responded. Then I almost crashed into one of the other candidates.

"Excuse me. Candidate coming through." Katia Newbaum walked past me with four other students. They were carrying a giant diorama made of milk cartons, paper towel rolls, and aluminum foil.

"It's my vision for the school of the future," she informed me and kept walking. "Vote for Katia!"

"Good. I see . . . you've . . . met . . . some . . . of the . . . competition," Stevie said as he wheeled up behind me. "I've been . . . working . . . on a . . . slogan."

He explained that the initials of the Krelboyne Independent Party form K.I.P. His slogan?

"K.I.P. . . . Is . . . Hip," he smiled. "Not . . . bad, huh?"

Okay, Krelboynes are anything but hip, but it was better than others I'd heard already: "Krelboynes: Not Just for Science Anymore" and "Krelboynes Shall Inherit the Earth."

Before agreeing on a slogan, though, we had to go down to The Office and officially sign me up as a candidate. I'd been working on signing a phony name, but they'd probably catch me at it. And if I pretended I had multiple personalities, I'd be out of the election and into therapy.

Again.

I decided I'd rather sign up. After all, somebody has to be pro-Krelboyne. I just wish it wasn't me.

We sat at The Office and waited. And waited. And waited. Finally, a hunched little man who was anywhere from like a thousand years old to a million thousand came out with a stack of folders. He plopped them on the counter in front of me and Stevie.

"Sign here, please." He shoved a tattered index card toward us.

"What . . . is . . . it?" Stevie asked.

"It says you'll read these election bylaws and return them by tomorrow."

"Tomorrow?" I'm a genius, not a speed reader. What is this guy *thinking*?

"Other students are running and they have to read them, too," he explained.

"What? I don't even get my own copy?"

"You think the school is made of money?" he asked in that way that means he doesn't want an answer. "Photocopying costs. This is a school for sharing."

Stevie made a note: "Referendum number 1: Next election, each candidate gets his own copy of the rules."

Minutes later, Stevie and I sat in the library and sorted through the pile of paperwork. Who knew a lame school election had so many rules and regulations? Stuff about assembling, meetings, campaign promises, where to hang banners and signs, the proper use of thumbtacks and staplers and all that junk.

And then I saw it. The most embarrassing piece of paper in the pile . . .

CHAPTER FIVE

"**D**ear INSERT PARENT'S NAME HERE. Please allow INSERT STUDENT'S NAME HERE to run for INSERT NAME OF OFFICE HERE . . ." my mom read at the dinner table.

"A permission slip?" Reese laughed so hard a piece of Hamburger Helper shot out his nose.

I need a note from my parents to run for a school office I didn't want to run for in the first place.

The only thing I want to run for now is cover.

I'd held on to the note for days, hoping that it would go away, or that I would lose it somehow, but Stevie kept asking about it. Now that it's Friday, I have no choice but to bring it home and get a signature.

"I think it's nice that your class thought so much of you to nominate you," Mom said. She inserted the appropriate names and signed the bottom. "I knew being a Krelboyne would be good for you."

Good for me? Brussels sprouts are good for me and I hate those, too.

"A student election is a wonderful thing," Dad said. He's always saying things like that. "It'll give you confidence, make you popular. Unless you lose, of course."

"What happens then?" I asked.

"You're better off not knowing," Dad replied.

"Malcolm needs a note from his mommy!" Reese chuckled and pointed.

"Mom!" I begged.

"Reese, be quiet. At least your brother's trying to make something of himself."

Yeah. Make myself a target for humiliation.

"Can I have a note, too?" Dewey asked.

"When you're older, honey," Mom replied.

"I remember *my* days in student government," Dad said. "Oh, the fun we had. We'd get together in the gym and paint banners that we would hang all over the school . . ."

Great. Another boring dinnertime story about the "glory days." Mom's happy and Dad's telling a story. Only one thing to do: escape.

The doorbell rang.

"I'll get it!" I dropped the plastic container of potato salad and slid from the table. I was out of the kitchen and running for the front door before Reese could lift his spoon.

When I opened the door, I saw . . . heaven. I mean Heather. Heather Gilstratten.

"Hello, Malcolm," she purred. No, I mean it. She sounded just like a little kitten. An adorable little kitten, standing in my doorway.

"Uh, hi, Heather," I replied. Note to brain: Please help now! Must have clever conversation. "What's up?" So far so good. Thanks, brain.

Heather was older than me. I think Reese had actually talked to her before. With her long black hair and pretty green eyes, she is much too cute to be talking to me. But who am I to question good luck when it knocks on my front door?

"You're running for Class President?" she asked.

"Yeah, I am." Hey, this student government thing is looking okay.

"I'm having a problem with my History grade, and maybe I could vote for you if, once you're, like, the President, y'know, you could get the school to change it. A totally nice C+ or even a B-. Something like that. So I can get into, like, a good Junior college."

Wow. That was fast. I'm not even in office yet, and already I'm being offered my first bribe?

"I've always thought you were passably cute," she added.

Bribery *and* flattery. She's good. And did I mention cute? Like a kitten?

She waited for an answer. I felt my heart race a thousand "yeses" to my mouth. But my brain was faster and a single "no" fell out ahead of them. It was followed by, "We're in different grades. You can't vote for me."

"Fine!" she snarled. "I'll just vote for someone who cares about *me*!" The kitten was gone and in her place was a tiger. A vicious, biting tiger.

"Hey! Young master Malcolm!" a voice cried from the sidewalk.

Francis! He's home! Saved! The tiger won't kill me in front of a witness.

"Hi, Francis!" I yelled from the porch. "Wait 'til I tell you what's been going on!"

Francis climbed up the steps and into the doorway. Heather moved slightly to let him pass.

"Hello, Francis," she purred to my brother. Now she was a kitten again? Girls.

"Heather," Francis said as he passed right by her. He went straight for the kitchen, calling out. "Hey, is that Hamburger Helper I smell?"

CHAPTER SIX

"**W**ould young master President Malcolm please pass me a spoon?" Francis said as Reese giggled.

"Yes, Mr. President. I'd like a spoon, too," Reese mocked.

"You want a spoon, too?" I asked my little brother.

"No thank you, Mr. Lincoln," Dewey said. He liked to suck his butterscotch pudding through a hole in the bottom.

Dinner was over. Dad was asleep in front of the television, Mom was doing laundry, and Dewey was in his underwear. He had managed to spill most of his dinner on his clothes, which is why mom was doing laundry.

In other words, just another Friday night at my house.

"I remember my campaign for Class President," Francis said. "The sirens, the police, the fire department, the tear gas, the television reporters. It was a very eventful election day."

"Dude, you were grounded for months!" Reese remembered proudly. "It's still a family record."

"If you want my help, Malcolm, all you have to do is ask," Francis said.

"Thanks, but I want to win without getting arrested," I said.

"Hey, a win's a win," Francis said. "But if you change your mind, I'll be back in two weeks."

"In two weeks?" I gasped. "How can you come home again so quickly?"

Francis reached into his pocket and pulled out two small rectangles of paper. Concert tickets! "To Dead Trout," he said. "I'm taking Gillian."

Reese was speechless, which was relatively easy for him. But I was speechless, too. Dead Trout is the hottest alternative band. Ever. They're not a pretty "boy band," and they don't sing gross songs about lost love and together forever and stupid stuff like that. They just thrash their instruments to great beats. And lyrics about fish. But I'm pretty sure that's just symbolism? For something.

"How . . . how did you get them?" I finally burbled.

"I won them," he said.

"How?"

"Doing something."

"Where?"

"Someplace."

Wow. Francis is so cool. And vague. I hope I can be that cool and vague when I'm older.

"How did you get Mom to agree?" I asked.

Francis didn't respond. In fact, he flinched. That could only mean one thing: Get ready for . . . a lie.

*　　*　　*

"So it was her dying wish that you go to the con-cert, huh?" Mom quizzed Francis as she filled the dryer with Dewey's clothes. She sniffed the wrinkled Cling Free sheet.

"Still got a few more tumbles left in it," she an-nounced as she threw it back in. We'd all gathered in the doorway. She slammed the dryer and switched it on. "All right. You can come home that weekend to go to the concert," she said to Francis. Then she paused.

I knew that pause. Francis knew it, too. There was about to be a catch. A *big* catch.

"You've got two tickets. That's one for you . . ." she paused again. "And a ticket for one of your brothers. It'll be good to get one of them out of the house for a night."

"But . . ." Francis started to say.

"Take it or leave it," Mom declared. Negotiations were closed tighter than the dryer door.

Yes! Dead Trout here I come! You think I'm too ea-ger? Well, Francis *has* to pick me over Reese. One, I'm the biggest Dead Trout fan. Like, ever! I've down-loaded tons of their music from the Internet. Or shouldn't I say that?

Anyway, two, Francis isn't embarrassed to be seen with me in public. That's huge. And three, and this is the big one, he's *less* likely to end up in jail if he takes me.

"That's what I really wanted to do," Francis grinned

to Mom through his gritted teeth. It might have really been a grimace, but I didn't care. I was too busy dancing around the house.

Reese ran out and returned with a pair of bedroom slippers. He slid them on Francis's feet.

"Are these Dad's slippers?" Francis asked.

"He'll never miss them," Reese explained. "Now just make yourself comfortable, favorite brother Francis. Let me get you a hot towel."

"Anyone seen my slippers?" Dad called out from the living room.

This was going to get ugly.

CHAPTER SEVEN

"**C**artoons!" Reese yelled.

"Wrestling!" I yelled back. This was how we spent our Saturday mornings: arguing over what to watch on television.

"Cartoons!"

"Wrestling!"

"Morning." Francis entered the living room rubbing his sleepy eyes.

I yanked the remote from Reese and handed it to Francis. "I changed the batteries. It works almost half the time now."

Reese ran to the sofa and started arranging the cushions. "Sit here, Francis. You'll be more comfortable."

Francis clicked the TV to his favorite sports channel, and soon we were all watching elephant soccer from Thailand.

Before the first commercial, Francis was surrounded by a bowl of primary color M&M's (I picked out all the other ones), a plate of nachos, and some cold pizza that had been cut into bite-sized bits, each one with a different-colored toothpick in it. I fanned Francis with a folded newspaper. Reese massaged Francis's feet.

Dad walked past carrying a book of crossword puzzles. "What are you boys doing?" he asked.

"Worshipping," I answered.

"Well, that's fine. Don't hurt anyone." And then Dad disappeared into the bathroom with his puzzles. With a number 2 pencil, he'll be in there for hours, enjoying his "Away Time."

"How about a soda, Francis?" Reese held up a fresh can of diet. He took a sip and swirled it around in his mouth. "Perfect temperature."

"Dude, you drank out of *my* can," Francis pointed out.

Reese spit the soda back in the can. He handed it to Francis. "Good as new."

"Never mind. Suddenly I'm not thirsty anymore." He started to pick at his left ear.

"You need to clean it?" I asked.

"Let me get that for you!" Reese demanded.

Reese and I looked at each other and then took off to the bathroom in search of Q-Tips. That's when Mom called out.

"Malcolm! Telephone!" she screamed.

"Not now! Busy!" I replied.

"It's Stevie Kenarban and you will talk to him. He's a little crippled boy and the phone is his lifeline. Whatever you're doing can wait."

It's useless to argue when Mom talks like that. So I didn't try. I ran to the phone as Reese raced up the stairs.

"Malcolm . . ." Stevie gasped. "We've . . . got . . . to . . . work . . . on . . . the campaign."

"Stevie. I can't. I've got something more important to do. Let's do it later." I dropped the phone to the ground and ran toward the stairs. Reese was coming down.

"No Q-Tips," he said glumly.

"There weren't *any* in the bathroom?" I asked.

A light went on in Reese's head. "Bathroom! Of course!" He raced back up the stairs. I was already two steps ahead of him. Until he yanked my feet and ran over me as I slid down the stairs.

I was quick enough to grab his right shoe and twist it. Unfortunately, he landed on his head, which never slows him down.

We both made it to the bathroom door and pushed it open. Reese ransacked the drawers while I scanned the medicine cabinet.

Nothing. No Q-Tips. Lots of ointments, pills, and strangely colored liquids that Mom makes us drink every time we cough. Reese reached around the drain cleaner, the crusty old sponges, and the rust stains.

"Got it!" he cried.

He held out an old, discolored Q-Tip that looked like it had been used to clean a donkey's ears. He wiped it on his pants.

"He'll never know," Reese said. Then he pointed out the window. "Look over there."

I looked. How does he make me do that?

Reese pushed me into the bathtub and ran down the stairs. I sat in the tub feeling the back of my head for a bump.

"Malcolm?" Dad started. "What's a six-letter word for onomatopoeia?"

"Cuckoo!" I shouted, and ran out the door.

"Ahhhh. Of course."

Reese may have found a used Q-Tip, but I had a secret weapon.

Dewey.

I ran outside where Dewey was playing. He's always got Q-Tips. A ninety-nine-cent box can keep him busy for hours. Get this: Q-Tips are the only thing he *doesn't* stick in his ears.

"Welcome to Q-Tip Town," he greeted me. "Are you a monster?"

I grabbed a Q-Tip from a pile on the ground. "I need a volunteer. For a secret mission."

Dewey screamed. "The monster took the mayor!"

I ran into the living room, where Reese was already waiting. He held up his scraggly Q-Tip. I held up the mayor of Q-Tip Town.

Francis waved us off. "I'm sorry, Gillian," he said into the phone. "It's not *my* idea. I'll make it up to you."

It's tough to break a date with a girl. It takes a lot of effort to get one, so breaking it can't be good.

There was silence from Francis while he got what sounded like an earful from the other end.

"Who's this Jimmy guy?" Francis asked. "How did *he* get tickets?"

Still more silence.

"Hello? Hello?" Francis said into the lifeless phone. He tossed the phone to the sofa.

"I'm sad, my brothers," he said. "Entertain me."

Reese started dancing. Either that or he was doing an impression of the thumbless red colobus monkeys we'd seen on the Discovery Channel. I picked up some tennis balls and started juggling.

The balls got away from me pretty quickly. I forgot that I don't know how to juggle. They rolled under Reese's feet and he crashed to the ground.

"Boys! No fighting!" Mom cried out from upstairs.

"It wasn't me!" Reese and I shouted.

"Don't think I won't ground the both of you," Mom shouted back.

Francis's eyes widened and he snapped his fingers. We fell silent. "New plan," he said. "Something different. As much as I appreciate the groveling you're both doing, I'm starting to feel smothered. I need something to amuse me instead. A *challenge* for the two of you. A test. And whoever passes the test will get my extra ticket."

"How about I just beat up Malcolm and you give me the ticket because he's in the hospital eating through a straw?" Reese offered.

"Okay. That's an idea," Francis said after a little too much thought.

I turned to Reese. "How about I just pour syrup and gum in your hair while you're sleeping?" Physically, he's stronger. No doubt about that. But he has to sleep sometime.

"What kind of gum?" Reese asked.

"Those are both swell ideas," Francis interrupted. "However, I've come up with something a bit more . . . challenging."

This sounded evil. I liked it already.

CHAPTER EIGHT

I t's a contest. Not like one of those "Who can eat the most sugar-coated Quacks?" contests that Francis is famous for. Or the "Guess where my underwear is?" game that Dewey plays.

It's a *real* contest. A test of skill, cunning, and, dare I say it, genius that will have Reese and me at each other's throats for two weeks. It's the kind of contest that even when it's all over, Reese and I will hold a grudge against each other until puberty ends.

Now *that's* a competition!

"This is a game that originated many hundreds of years ago," Francis explained. "Possibly by the Yanomami on the banks of the Orinoco River in Venezuela. I've heard this game called many things. Some call it 'Not Me!' while others prefer 'He Did It! I Saw Him.' I call it by its original name: 'The Great Frame Game.'"

I looked at Reese. He was practically salivating — like when he sees a Pop-Tart.

"You have two weeks," Francis continued. "Each of you must try your best to frame the other — to get him grounded. Whichever of you isn't grounded by the weekend of the concert will get to see Dead Trout with yours truly."

Grounded. No phone calls. No social interaction. No television. No playing outside. You can only leave the house to go to school in the morning, and you have to return as soon as school lets out. And it can last for a day, several days, or a lifetime, depending on what you're getting blamed for.

"Let's go over the rules," Francis said. "Nothing gets broken. That's rule number 1." He turned to me. "So stay away from dishes and windows and Dad's old disco albums."

Francis turned to Reese. "And you, Reese, have to stay away from Malcolm's arms and legs. Also, neither of you can burn anything or steal anything."

Reese started to laugh as if he'd already won.

"Say good-bye to Dewey," Reese whispered sinisterly to me.

"And leave Dewey alone," Francis quickly added.

"Awww. You're taking the fun out of this already," Reese moaned and slumped.

No way! This was going to be *too* easy.

"All right, then," Francis said. "We're all clear on the rules?" He looked at us both. "Right?"

"Absolutely," Reese said.

"Oh yes," I replied. "*Very* clear."

Francis looked at his watch. "Then, the countdown begins. Three ... two ... one ... go!"

Reese and I bolted from the room in separate directions. It was time to put my plan into motion. I'd probably get Reese grounded before he'd even thought of his plan. My mind raced frantically as I thought about what to try first.

I went to the computer and started surfing the 'net for some ideas. I suddenly got an Instant Message from Stevie. "Malcolm for President??????" he wrote, but I didn't have time for it. I've got to win that ticket. I hit the "cancel" key.

When the message blipped away, that's when it hit me. Hard. Like a pop quiz in Algebra when I'd spent the day studying Ancient Arctic History and Folklore. Think about this: If I'm off doing something to get Reese in trouble, then he's off somewhere trying to get *me* in trouble. I didn't like that thought, so I walked carefully back into the living room to keep an eye on Reese.

Reese must have had the same thought. He was also carefully creeping back into the living room, checking to see if I had something hidden behind my back. We both sat on the couch.

Reese glared at me. I glared at Reese.

For several hours.

Francis is evil when he wants to be.

Francis is so cool.

This Great Frame Game is going to be way longer than our best game of I Dare You! and of Crap-gammon.

And this is sneakier and more evil. Who's gonna watch my back and ref-eree? Mom? Dad? I can't tell them. They'd ground me right away and then I'd lose the contest.

I could tell Dewey, but he'd either forget or repeat it to Mom and Dad. "Hi Mom, hi Dad, Malcolm's gonna try to get Reese grounded." That would never work.

So I'm on my own.

But what to do? How can I frame Reese for something if he's watching me 24-7 and I'm doing the same to him?

And then there's the election! Ste-vie's counting on me. The Krelboynes are counting on me. And in their own

weird way, my parents are even excited about it.

This is harder than those word problems about two trains going to different cities at different times. I'll
figure something out, though. Otherwise, I'll be campaigning while following
Reese around trying to stop him from
framing me.

And I don't even like to be in the
same room with him.

CHAPTER NINE

"**I**'m sorry, Stevie. I forgot."

Really! I did! I was going to call him, or even e-mail him, but I lost track of the time over the three-day holiday weekend.

Some holiday. Instead of reading comic books or being outside playing street hockey, Reese and I spent all of Sunday and Monday staring at each other, waiting for the other one to make a move. As a result, neither of us moved. So I couldn't go over to Stevie's even if I *had* remembered. I wasn't letting Reese out of my sight.

I even set my alarm clock for every fifteen minutes last night so I could check on him. He did the same. So he could check his hair for gum and syrup, of course.

I totally forgot that I was supposed to go over to Stevie's and plot out a strategy for my presidential campaign.

"Sorry?" he wheezed. "You're . . . always . . . sorry."

"Why didn't you call me?" I asked. "You have a phone."

"I did . . . call . . . you," he gasped. "You . . . hung up . . . on me."

"You could've called back —" I looked at Stevie. He wasn't buying it.

"And ... you ... ignored ... my IM."

He had me there. Thank you, technology, for making it too hard to lie. "Maybe you should have tried harder," I sputtered. "You *are* my campaign manager, after all."

"I shouldn't ... have to ... remind ... you to ... be my ... friend."

Okay. So *that* hurt. And it hurt enough for me to say something back.

"Look, Stevie, it's just a stupid election," I blurted. "Truth is, I don't care if I win or lose."

That was bad, but then I added, "I don't even care if I come in last."

Oops. Did I say all that out loud? Judging by the look on Stevie's face, I did. That is like the totally wrong thing to say to your campaign manager.

"That ..." he gasped, "does it!"

He spun his wheelchair around and turned his back on me. I can't really blame him. I was pretty harsh, I guess. I walked around to face him and that's when he let loose.

He told me that being nominated to run for President was an honor. It was something I should be proud of. They hadn't picked just any Krelboyne to be their nominee. They had picked me. My rejection of the nomination was a rejection of them ... and him.

Or so he said. Only it took him like a week to wheeze it out.

He was right, of course. And I did feel bad. I didn't even *want* to run, but everyone wants me to. Everyone is counting on me. Honestly, I was kinda getting into it. The whole election thing was starting to be fun.

So if I have to run for President, I'm going to need Stevie's help. I was about to apologize to him and make everything better when a drone from The Office walked up to us.

He had a note in his hand. I recognized it right away. You don't get to be my age without recognizing a piece of paper that has trouble written all over it.

"Which one of you is Malcolm?" the drone asked.

Stevie quickly pointed at me.

"You're wanted in The Office," he said.

See? Told you I recognized the note. I turned to Stevie. I wanted to get this settled so we could get back to running my campaign.

"Stevie? I — " I started.

"I . . . hope . . . you . . . fry." He wheeled to the other side of the classroom.

I guess I deserved that. You know, the last time I got called to The Office, I ended up a Krelboyne. This can't be any worse than that.

Can it?

CHAPTER TEN

'm starting to like The Office. It has a cozy, warm feeling. There are no teachers here. There are certainly no Krelboynes, and I can hear some okay music coming from someone's radio. If they had a refrigerator and a Playstation, I could easily spend the rest of my life here.

I have totally no idea what they want with me.

"Uh, hi," I said to the secretary. "I'm Malcolm —"

She just pointed down the hallway to the door at the end.

Uh-oh. I knew where this was going.

I entered the room. It was filled with pictures of rainbows and nature scenes. I swear I heard birds chirping.

"Hello, Miss Gilbert," I greeted. "I'm reporting for my sanity checkup." Miss Gilbert is the school shrink. The therapist. The last time I saw her, I was just acting weird to get out of Medieval Week.

"Malcolm, I thought we had been making progress since our last session several weeks ago," she said sweetly.

"Yes. Me too."

"But then something like this comes along and I worry that you're slipping."

My mind raced. What had I done? What was I being blamed for? Did I make a strange campaign promise? Did I put my posters on the wrong wall? Wait! I didn't put posters on any wall! She's leading up to something. I don't know what, but with a buildup like this, it's got to be huge.

She pulled out a cardboard box.

"We got an anonymous call this morning and found these in your locker," she said as she pulled out a blond wig, a woman's nightgown, some fuzzy pink bedroom slippers, and an old copy of Vogue. They were my mom's.

Anonymous tip? Leave it to Reese to be totally obvious.

"I know that being an advanced student in a special class and running for President of your grade can be very stressful," she offered. "Sometimes we can't handle those stresses. We cry out for help." She paused. "Do you need that help, Malcolm?"

"No. I'm fine. Really." The only help I need is how to get back at my brother.

She put the stuff back in the box. "We're going to keep this as our little secret, Malcolm," she said. "And let's not let this happen again. You know, whenever you're ready for that help, my door is always open."

That's a comfort. What I really want to do is slam that open door on my lame brother. He's playing dirty. Dirty and lame.

He's going to pay.

CHAPTER ELEVEN

"*S*tevie!"

"Malcolm!"

"Stevie!"

"Malcolm!"

I was thinking how to explain my Office visit to Stevie — I was picking up an official "election kit" or something equally lame. Then I heard the yelling from the Krelboyne trailer.

What I saw inside was even weirder. The Krelboynes had split into two groups. They were yelling at each other like parents at a Little League game.

As soon as I entered the room, the people who were yelling my name started to cheer. The others started to boo.

Stevie wheeled over to me and handed me a piece of paper. It was his resignation as my campaign manager.

"I'm . . . now . . . the best . . . man . . . for . . . the job," Stevie said.

I guess it's too late to apologize to him now. While I was at the office defending myself against Reese's underhanded tactics, Stevie had taken matters in his own hands.

He was so upset by what I said to him that he split off from the Krelboyne Independent Party and formed the Krelboyne *Progressive* Party. And he's *their* nominee for Class President. That's right. My former campaign manager is now my opponent.

"You . . . are . . . going . . . down!" Stevie wheezed.

"Stevie for President!" his supporters roared and gathered around him.

"Malcolm for President!" somebody screamed out.

Dabney and Lloyd patted me on the back. Eraserhead shook my hand and said, "We're with you all the way, Malcolm!"

"This is our first step toward a national third party," Lloyd said. "Next stop, the White House!"

It looks like it's Stevie against me. Progressives against Independents. Krelboyne against Krelboyne. Nerd against — wait, maybe I better quit while I'm ahead.

"C'mon, Stevie," Clyde said. "Let's get you properly registered and we can formulate a strategy." Clyde and Stevie turned to exit. "I'm *his* campaign manager," Clyde bragged as they went through the door. "*And* I've memorized the periodic table. By atomic weight."

After that, things got a little heated in the classroom. The two sides moved closer and closer and the insults flew back and forth.

"Cro-Magnon!"

"Your father hasn't finished his doctoral thesis yet!"

"You're not going to get into an Ivy League school!"

"Your mother's SAT score was only fifteen-eighty-five!"

Okay, so maybe those don't count as real insults, but they were harsh enough to make more than a few Krelboynes cry.

By the time the teacher restored order, no one was speaking to anyone. Which was fine by me.

I looked around the classroom. Dabney, Lloyd, and Eraserhead were each holding up signs they'd made out of notebook paper. "I want to be your new campaign manager," each read. The trio pointed to themselves and nodded.

Great.

But they were right. If I'm going to beat Stevie and win this thing, I need some help. Serious help. I wonder what Francis is doing right now?

CHAPTER TWELVE

*N*ext morning, I smelled trouble. Maybe it's just me, but trouble always seems to start as soon as I get up. Maybe I should start sleeping late.

The living room was a total mess of paper. Dad sat in the middle of it. This is what happens when you allow your family to help.

"Good morning, sport," he said cheerily. "What d'you think?" He held up a banner that read "MALCOLM IS NUMERO UNO!" "I've got some others, too."

Sure enough, my dad had made banners and signs with all sorts of slogans. "VOTE FOR MALCOLM." "MALCOLM IS THE BEST." "MALCOLM WANTS YOUR VOTE." "A VOTE FOR MALCOLM IS A VOTE FOR DEMOCRACY."

He did have one I really liked: "MALCOLM IS THE MAN." It had a nice, catchy ring to it. And it made me sound more mature.

See, I tried calling Francis, but he was too busy faking appendicitis to get out of a ten-mile hike. Plus, since Reese and I were competing for his extra ticket, he didn't want to show favoritism.

Dewey pushed his way out from underneath a huge pile of paper. "I have some slow gums, too," he offered. "'MALCOLM IS MAGIC LIKE SANTA' and 'MALCOLM LIKES CHEESE.'"

At least he's trying. Then I smelled the burning. I ran into the kitchen. There was no fire, only Mom standing next to the microwave. "Good morning," she said. Then she added the most terrifying words I've ever heard since "Give your aunt a kiss."

"I baked cookies for your campaign, Malcolm." Inside my head, I was screaming. But the only word that came out was, "Thanks."

I totally appreciated the effort, but my mom follows a recipe like Reese does geometry. Sure, there are a bunch of shapes and pictures, but in the end, it doesn't add up to anything tasty.

I was hoping she would just buy something for me to hand out to voters or go a whole week without yelling at me. That's the kind of help I could really use. But her special homemade cookies?

The microwave dinged and she took them out. At least they didn't look too bad — kind of like sugar-coated charcoal.

Reese strolled into the kitchen, looking confused. "Hey, how come the lights are on? I saw Malcolm —"

"Forget it, Reese," I whispered. "I put all the fuses back in the fuse box. And I got Dad's chair back from Mr. Fieldcrest."

"Oh, yeah?" Reese chuckled. "Well, I picked up all Mom's clothes that you threw on the lawn. And I got my headphones out of the garbage disposal."

I'd had a busy night. Reese was *not* going to win

that ticket. I'd have to keep a closer watch on him. That meant it was time for plan B.

Plan B was very simple: Watching television with Reese and not letting him out of my sight. But I'm sitting on the sofa and it totally dawns on me: Reese isn't here. I've been watching *Cops Goes to Montana* by myself.

Reese was gone. You know what that means? He's out plotting, scheming, and planning to the fullest extent that his hamster brain can manage. I rocketed off the sofa as if I'd sat on a porcupine.

I searched the house. Not necessarily frenetically, but a word that means the same thing. I looked in the bedrooms, the bathroom, the kitchen, the living room, in the clothes hamper (which is Dewey's favorite hiding place), and even under the kitchen sink. Nothing. No Reese. I did find Dewey in a closet protecting his Q-Tips.

"Keep away, monster," he yelled. Then he threw his little body over a pile of cotton-tipped villagers. I closed the door . . .

And heard a chainsaw.

Or someone trying to start a chainsaw. I ran to the backyard and what I saw could only be described as astounding. Reese stood on top of the minivan, ready to cut it in half.

"Reese! No!" I cried.

"Francis didn't say we couldn't cut stuff in two!" Reese replied, referencing the rules of the game.

Reese yanked the starter cord and . . . nothing. No metal teeth ripping into Detroit steel. No crying parents yelling my brother's name.

"Oh, man," he cursed. "Out of gas."

"Where's my jump rope?" Dad bellowed as he wandered through the house. "I distinctly remember leaving it next to my *Saturday Night Fever* album and my wristbands."

Let him wonder, because I'm *not* losing the contest. Reese and I were now tied together, three feet apart, by my dad's old jump rope.

"You're not leaving my sight, Reese," I said. "Not for one minute, not for one second, not for any reason."

Reese grinned evilly. "I have to go the bathroom."

Okay. Maybe one reason.

I stood outside the bathroom while Reese went in and closed the door. We were still attached by the rope, of course. I had my fingers in my ears, because who wants to hear anything, right? Then I realize he's been in there for like fifteen whole minutes. Only a dad can spend that much time on the toilet.

Against my better judgment, I opened the door. Then I opened my eyes. The other end of the rope lay on the floor. Reese was gone. He'd climbed out the window.

The last I saw of him, he was running down the street, carrying the chainsaw, looking for a gas station.

CHAPTER THIRTEEN

"And . . . I . . . promise to . . . cut . . . taxes . . ."

Somehow Stevie thinks making promises like that will get him votes? We're in school! The only thing taxing is listening to him make speeches. If Stevie promises to stop doing that, he's got *my* vote.

The school totally looks like it's Christmas, but instead of decking the halls with boughs of holly, they're plastered with Stevie's giant face on posters with sayings like "VOTE FOR STEVIE KENARBAN AND HE'LL CUT TAXES."

What's with the taxes?

What about no PE? No grades? TV Appreciation Class? You know, the *important* things in life. That's what I'd be promising.

"And what are you promising?" some kid asked me. "Stevie says he's going to cut —"

"I know! I know!" I retorted.

These are the moments in life when you really, really wish you didn't have to go to school. Wait, that's every moment in life. But this is especially one of those moments. The kid and his friends stared at me like I was a monkey about to do tricks or something. I knew they were waiting for my campaign promise, so I had to make it something good.

"I promise . . ." I began. More kids gathered around me to hear what the Krelboyne Independent Party candidate had to say. "To . . ." I continued. More kids packed around me. "To . . ."

"Maybe he'll cut more taxes," one kid whispered to another.

". . . To order new textbooks for the English classes."

A pack of blank faces stared at me in silence. I need a save! Something quick! Something to get them excited. Something . . .

"And have a two-hour lunch." Before I knew what I was saying, I said it. Two hours for lunch? I didn't have the power to add two minutes. But there it was, like an ugly pimple on my chin. Not much I could do about it now except hope it goes away before someone notices.

Before I could take it back, the pack of kids bolted away like they were exploding from a grenade. "Two-hour lunch! Two-hour lunch!" They ran off quacking like ducks and cheered me. "Malcolm rules! Malcolm rules!"

I rule? Maybe I could get to like this. Then, as the crowd parted, I saw Stevie leering at me.

"How are . . . you going . . . to do . . . that?" he growled.

"I have connections," I answered.

Connections? Right. The only connections I can make are in Dewey's connect-the-dots book.

"So . . . you've got . . . the principal . . . in your . . . pocket?" Stevie assumed. "Two . . . can play . . . at that . . . game."

Stevie rolled away with Clyde. Clyde immediately whipped out a pad and pencil and scribbled notes while Stevie wheezed instructions. Clyde scribbled and pencil lead flew. They were serious.

As quickly as Stevie left, the fellow members of "my" Krelboyne Independent Party swooped down and surrounded me. The day had started out so well. Now I'm playing "Ring-Around-the-Malcolm" with the Pocket Protector Police.

I'm sure they're concerned about something lame like maximizing the Krelboyne Independent Party's exposure through a diversified platform featuring a multitiered approach to pivotal issues.

What? Like *I* understand it?

"We'd like to discuss your strategies with you, Malcolm," Flora said.

"What strategies?" I asked.

"Exactly," Flora replied with a curl in her lip.

"In case you haven't noticed, the school's been re-decorated in a lovely shade of STEVIE'S FACE!" Lloyd whined.

"Do I have to do everything?" I hissed.

"You haven't done *anything*!" Flora loudly pointed out.

"That's not true! I've done a lot of things. They just aren't as obvious as Stevie's giant face."

To be honest, I could count the things I've done for this campaign on one hand. One finger, actually.

"Well, maybe one of you could help or something!" I shot back.

Lloyd cleared his throat. "We're the support staff. We're not supposed to be working on the front lines. That's what the campaign manager is for. Do you even *have* a campaign manager?"

Yeah, I had one once, but now he's running against me. Duh! Where has Lloyd been for the last two days?

The Krelboynes waited for my response, which would have been "I quit," but Eraserhead raced up and broke through the circle. He fell into Flora's arms and gasped for breath like a fish washed up on the shore.

"What is it?" Flora implored.

"Ste ... Ste ... Ste ..." Eraserhead stammered between heaving breaths. Lloyd took out his asthma inhaler and slapped it into Eraserhead's mouth. Eraserhead took a deep breath and collapsed onto the floor. We circled around him like vultures.

"Stevie!" Eraserhead shouted.

"Yeah, we got that part," I said.

"He's saying Malcolm cheated on his IQ test!"

"Oh, yeah. Like I *wanted* to be a Krelboyne," I replied, rolling my eyes. If I had known scoring so well was going to put me in the Krelboyne class,

Stevie's right, I would've cheated — and failed on purpose.

"And," Eraserhead continued, "Stevie's claiming you embezzled campaign funds!"

"Embezzled campaign funds?" I laughed. "There are no campaign funds."

Lloyd gave me a sideways look. "What happened to them?"

"What do you mean, 'What happened to them?' There never were any!" I defended.

"A likely story," Lloyd huffed and placed a hand over the wallet in his back pocket.

What's Stevie doing with these lies? I know he's mad, but this is nuts. He's firing ammo like this is a war — and now that I think about it? Maybe it is. I was going to quit, but if I do now, it'll look like Stevie's telling the truth. If Stevie's looking for a fight, he's got one.

"You want a strategy," I said to the Krelboynes. "Here's your strategy ..." They huddled closer — except Lloyd, who wanted to keep his money far from me. "We're bringing Stevie down."

Great. Now what? Am I supposed to go around telling people Stevie can really walk and only uses his chair to get the sympathy vote? I'd just be sinking to his level. I know that sounds like the first thing I'd do, but maybe that can be my backup plan.

Flora suggested I promise to abolish homework. Yeah, right. I'd have a better chance of getting everyone to the moon. I mean, homework is the very essence of school. It's the way teachers make you miserable long after you've left their classroom. They go home at night filled with happy thoughts about you slaving over chapter seven while they go bowling or play miniature golf or whatever teachers do when they aren't asking you who won the War of the Roses. There is no way they'd ever give up that control.

But I can't just sit back and let Stevie run away with this. Lloyd was right. I need a campaign manager. "Desperate times call for desperate measures." Someone a lot more famous than I'll ever be said that. I think it was George W. Bush.

No, I'm not going to spread lies about Stevie. I'm going to do something so bad, I don't even want to say it. Just thinking about it sends chills down my spine.

I'm going to ask Reese for help.

I know what you're thinking. Reese as my campaign manager at the same time he's trying to frame me? Isn't that a conflict of interest or something? I mean, if I'm trying to get Reese framed, too, how come I'm asking him for help with the election?

Well, I could say it's one way to keep an eye on him — at least I'll know where he is and what he's up to. Or I could be honest and just say I'm totally desperate.

Okay, I'm totally desperate.

And despite being born smart? I couldn't come up with a better solution.

That's my answer, but why would Reese agree to help the person he's trying to frame? Easy! I just appealed to his need to pound people. And besides, Reese doesn't know what conflict of interest means.

And even if he did, he'd still want to pound people.

CHAPTER FOURTEEN

It took up my whole lunch period, but I finally found him. I don't know what I was thinking. It's like that Dr. Frankenstein guy who made the Frankenstein monster. I mean, what was *that* dude thinking? Okay, so I'm not digging up body parts from cemeteries, but I might be creating a monster. But, I need Reese. He can influence the kids in ways that posters and promises never could.

Okay, maybe not influence so much as threaten. But a vote *is* a vote, right?

So how do you find someone like Reese when you're at school? Usually you listen for the screams of helpless children or go to the place that all the geeks are running away from. There were no running geeks this time, just running water.

Yeah, water. I found Reese in the boys' bathroom flooding the toilets. Water was totally covering the tile floor. I could hear Reese behind one of the stall doors, laughing. I'm not sure what he was laughing about. You could file that under "Too Much Info." I sloshed across the bathroom and knocked on the stall door.

"What? I'm busy!" Reese yelled from the other side.

Busy? Gross.

"Reese! It's me," I said back, hoping I wouldn't hear the toilet flush a final time.

The door creaked open and Reese squeezed out.

"What are you doing here?" he asked.

"We go to the same school."

Not that he'd ever know. I'm not allowed to talk to him when we're at school. And since I became a Krelboyne, if I need to talk to him, I have to tie a red flag to his locker; then he meets me in the bathroom that's farthest from the schoolyard. It's like some total spy thing. I'm surprised he doesn't make me sit in one stall while he sits in another and we talk through the middle wall. That'd just be creepy.

"I know we go to the same school, dipwad. Who could forget when your brother's a total embarrassment," he said, drying his hands on his shirt.

"Look, Reese, I need your help," I began.

Before I could say another word, Reese totally busted out in laughter. "You need . . . you need . . . you need my . . ." he babbled between laughs. He bent over and grabbed his stomach. Tears formed in his eyes, and he laughed so hard he fell over and plopped into the water covering the bathroom floor.

"This isn't easy for me, Reese." I was frustrated and wanted to get this whole thing over with.

"What's wrong? One of the Krelboynes picking on you, little bro?"

I knew he'd do this. Reese takes every chance to

humiliate me. Suddenly my idea was sounding totally twisted. I'm about to ask him for help *while*
we're trying to frame each other?

"Okay! Fine! It was a dumb idea! I don't need this!
And I don't need a stupid campaign manager, okay!"
I yelled at Reese, who was still on his back laugh-
ing.

Reese stopped laughing and jumped up from the
floor. Water soaked the back of his shirt. With his
dripping arm, he blocked me from leaving the bathroom.

"Did you say 'campaign manager'?" he asked.

"I need someone to help me beat Stevie in the election, okay? But I can see you're too busy flooding toilets or whatever it is you do when you can't hit
someone."

"Me? Campaign manager?" Reese asked again.
His eyes started to glaze over. That means he's
thinking. This could take a while.

Look what I've been reduced to. I made Reese
think. Standing in two inches of water with my
brother, asking for a favor. I should just drop out.
Quit. Call it a day. I'm outta here. See ya later. *Hasta
la vi —*"

"I'll do it," Reese finally said, his eyes rolling back
to normal. "I'll be your campaign manager."

"Great." I didn't know if I should laugh or cry.

"One thing. What does 'campaign manager' mean?"
Reese asked.

Cry. Definitely cry.

"It means I need you to . . . convince . . . people to vote for me instead of Stevie."

"Con . . . vince," Reese said, his eyes lighting up. "I like the sound of that."

Reese went in the toilet stall and gave it a final flush. More water flooded over the edge of the bowl and spilled on the floor. Then I saw it! The stall was filled with stuff that had my name on it! Books, homework, and even my school photo were scattered inside the stall.

"Welcome to Grounded City: population you!" Reese chortled and ran out of the bathroom.

"Flood! Flood! Flood in the bathroom!" I could hear him yell as he ran down the hallway.

CHAPTER FIFTEEN

"**H**ow do you explain *this*?" the principal asked as he tossed a pair of white underpants on his desk.

I picked up the underwear — *my* underwear — and shook my head. "I have no idea how these got in the flooded toilet stall."

Okay I lied. What was I supposed to say? Reese and I are trying to frame each other? I should've just said, "My brother's trying to destroy my life." The principal might've understood. He might have a brother, too.

"But that *is* your name in the waistband?" he inquired, as if he didn't know my name is Malcolm.

What's with adults always asking questions they already know the answers to? Is it a test, or are they just bored?

"I know this looks bad, sir . . ."

"Yes, it does. It may have to go down in your permanent record."

The permanent record. The ultimate threat. Worse than no dessert or cutting off TV, it's been the mythic shadow hanging over every kid's head since we rode to school in a covered wagon and lived on a prairie. Honestly? I don't even think they exist, but I'm not about to test that theory.

"I swear I didn't do it!" I pleaded.

It's always good to use words like "swear," "promise," and "honest" when denying anything. The fact that I'm telling the truth this time is only coincidental.

"Looking at your track record, I see that you've kept your nose out of trouble for the most part . . . except for that incident with the cow's liver and poor Mrs. Hagworth," the principal said.

Oh, man! He had to bring that one up? How many times does a kid have to say he's sorry? Besides, her insurance paid for everything.

"I'll let you slide this time with a week's detention," he added, standing up at his desk.

A week's detention? If that's sliding, I'd hate to see what the punishment would've been. But detention isn't grounding, so Reese still doesn't win Francis's extra concert ticket. One way or another, I'll get Reese back for this.

The state of my underwear quickly became the least of my problems. Ever had one of those bad dreams where you think you wake up, but you're really just in another bad dream?

Welcome to my life.

I walked from the principal's office — right into the face of bad dream number two.

"Meeting with . . . your . . . puppet again?" Stevie asked sarcastically, pointing to the principal's office.

"He's *not* my puppet," I defended.

Stevie rolled his eyes, then turned his wheelchair around and pushed away. I chased after him and leaped into his path.

"Don't . . . make . . . me . . . roll . . . you . . ."

"This is lame," I interrupted, not having the patience to wait until he finished.

"Over," he finished anyway.

"Why are you spreading lies about me, Stevie? You know I don't care about this stupid election."

"And . . . that's why . . . we're . . . fighting," Stevie continued. "This . . . was . . . important to . . . me . . . and you . . . didn't . . . care."

Ouch. I'll think of some really smart reply . . . just as soon as I pull the knife out of my back.

"Stevie, don't confuse my lack of enthusiasm for a . . . lack of . . . enthusiam." That sounded a lot better in my head.

"You . . . can . . . always . . . drop out," Stevie suggested.

"No way!" I exploded. "Then everyone will think I did it because you were telling the truth! I'm not a quitter."

"Aren't you?"

Whoa! Two knives, one back. He's getting better at this.

"This stinks, Stevie. If we're both going to run, let's make it a fair campaign. No lies. No tricks," I promised.

"And . . . no . . . puppets," Stevie said, motioning to the principal's office.

"You got it," I answered and extended my hand.

Stevie looked at me with his big round glasses, and I could tell that what I said had made sense to him. He thought for a moment, then slowly reached out to shake my hand.

The problem should have been solved. Stevie and I should have been opponents — and friends — again. The battle should have ended. Instead, that's when everything *really* turned rotten.

"Gaaaah!" some kid squealed as he ran past me and Stevie. His white underwear poked out several inches above his waistline.

Trouble.

A second kid ran by with his underwear hiked twice as high as the first one's. Only one person could deliver two massive wedgies like that in under a minute.

"There's more to come if you vote for Stevie the Wheelie!" Reese hissed as he bolted around the corner.

Stevie pulled his hand back faster than the wedgie victims fled Reese. "So . . . that's . . . how . . . it . . . is," Stevie said. "I . . . almost . . . believed . . . you."

"I swear I had no idea!" I whined back.

Maybe I should have used "honest" or "promise," 'cause Stevie didn't bite on the "swear." And I was telling the truth again. That's twice in one day! It was too late, though. Stevie just turned his chair and rolled away as Reese ran up to me.

"If I had known politics was this much fun, I'd be campaign manager every year!" Reese chortled.

Now I know how Dr. Frankenstein felt when his monster ran through the village.

CHAPTER SIXTEEN

'm staying in my room. It's the only safe place I have. You ever get that feeling? That outside everything is just crud, so why not stay in your room? It's got everything I need. CheezeBalls under the bed. A TV that sometimes works. Pillows. Video games. What more do I need? Sure, I *could* go out and talk to my family, but human contact is highly overrated. And Reese is out there somewhere, plotting his next attack to get me grounded. If I just stay in my room, I'm sure to be —

"Mallllcolm!"

I'm sure to be —

"Mallllcolm!" my mom shouted again.

There goes my night. I trudged from my fortress of solitude and into the kitchen where my mom waited with a load of laundry.

"Did you do this, Mister?" she barked.

"The laundry?" I asked.

"No! *This!*" She held up a small shirt. Did I say small? Make that tiny. Like, even a leprechaun would have to squeeze to fit into this thing.

"Someone put the dryer on 'High' and shrank all

the clothes!" Mom spat, pulling out a pair of Dad's pants that wouldn't fit Dewey now.

"Why do you think *I* did it?"

"Because," Mom continued, focusing all her will-power to remain calm. "The only clothes that were taken out of the dryer before they shrank were . . ."

She didn't even need to finish the sentence. I knew what was coming next, and I looked back over my shoulder to see how quickly I could run back to my room.

"Let me guess," I interrupted. "The only clothes taken out before they shrank were mine."

"Don't you think that's a little coincidental?"

It was more than coincidental. It was amazing. Reese actually knows how to use the clothes dryer. That's like those little lab rats that can find their way to the end of a maze. I don't know if I should be mad at Reese or give him a kibble treat.

"Now what am I supposed to do with these?" Mom yelled and threw the tiny clothing around the kitchen. "Sell them to circus freaks?"

I wish she'd sell me to circus freaks. Anything's better than this.

Before I could answer, the kitchen door swung open and my dad stomped in — or something that looked a lot like my dad stomped in. Usually my dad doesn't have egg splattered all over his head.

"Malcolm," he said in a calm voice. "Any chance you know how these eggs got on me?"

The old parental trick question. Sure my dad

asked, "Do you know?" but he really meant, "I know it was you." This is just a test parents like to throw out there to make you suffer. Then, if you lie, they love to follow up with things like "I gave you a chance to tell the truth."

I didn't throw the eggs. Of course, I knew who did it, but if I say it's Reese and he has an alibi, it'll just get me into hotter water.

While my dad wiped the egg off his face and got ready for some intense interrogation, the phone rang. Great. This was the break I needed to think of a plan to crush Reese. This should be easier than getting Dewey to stick something in his ear. I *am* a genius, after all. This is the kind of thing we geniuses are good at. Any second now the idea to end all ideas will pop into my head in a flash of genius inspiration. Yep. Any second now. Here it comes . . .

Nope, that wasn't it. Wait. Maybe this one . . . no. How about . . . *that's* got nothing to do with Reese.

You know what stinks about being a genius? Not only do you have class in a trailer, but everybody expects you to always have the best answers to everything. So you spend all your time thinking and thinking until you lose the ability to talk to a girl or dance or play any sport that doesn't have bishops and pawns, and I hate bishops and pawns because I know that the way things are going they'll be my only dates on Friday night for the rest of my genius life.

What was I supposed to be thinking about again?

"Malcolm! Reese! It's Francis. He wants to talk to you," Mom called out.

Francis? Cool! I ran to the phone and lifted it off the receiver. Reese's eager grunts greeted me. He was on an extension somewhere else in the house — probably with an empty egg carton in his lap.

"Young master Malcolm," Francis said. "Kind of you to join us. Reese has been telling me of his progress. Crude, yet effective."

"Yeah. He's been a real creative wizard," I said in a monotone voice.

"And what progress have you made in the great Frame Game?" Francis asked.

Francis was hoping to hear all the dirty details of my grand scheme. Some secret yet graceful plan that would fall like a giant row of dominos and crush Reese under the final piece.

"Well," I began, "I've kinda been busy at school with the election, and . . ."

"I see," Francis interrupted. "Afraid to show your hand with Reese on the phone."

Afraid to show my hand? The only hands I have should be choking Reese about now. Now *that's* an idea.

"Perhaps this will give you some incentive," Francis continued.

Francis moved the phone to his stereo and blasted the latest tune from Dead Trout. Even through the phone they sounded amazing.

Torture. That's all I can say. Seeing Dead Trout live

would be the ultimate, coolest thing that could happen to anyone. And here I am stuck in the middle of a stupid election with no best friend — it's hard to concentrate on the downfall of my brother to get those tickets.

What was I thinking?

CHAPTER SEVENTEEN

Students wandered around the lunch quad looking for something more interesting than the glob of foodstuff they were slopping on trays in the cafeteria. What they found wasn't really more interesting, but it was less likely to give them gas in sixth period.

It was the candidates shaking hands, making promises, handing out buttons. I'm sorry to say I was right there with them, wearing an ironed shirt for the first time since Grandma's wedding.

"Hi! Hello," I said from behind my campaign table, slapping a button into some blond kid's open hand.

"Ouch!" He yelped and threw down the button. "You jabbed me! You jabbed me!"

"Vote for Malcolm!" Eraserhead called out as the kid ran away in tears.

That's when I saw Stevie across the quad. He was smiling and shaking his head. I sneered back at him. Stevie was handing out cookies shaped like wheelchairs. "ROLL TO VICTORY" was written across each one in frosting.

I had cookies. Mom's cookies. I grabbed one from the shoebox.

"Here," I offered to another would-be voter.

The girl looked quizzically at the nuggetlike cookie. "What's it supposed to be? Stevie's look exactly like his wheelchair."

"It's an asteroid," I covered.

"An asteroid?"

"Just eat it, okay?"

The girl held the cookie like an apple and took a generous bite. Her eyes widened, followed by a gag. "Water . . ." she croaked and bolted for the water fountain.

I glanced at the remaining cookies. They started to look more like lumps than chocolate chips. I took my foot and slowly nudged the box under the table where they could do no more harm.

Other candidates dotted the quad as well. Each grade has its own would-be presidents, vice presidents, treasurers, secretaries, and whatever other lame offices make up student body government.

Next to Stevie's table was Katia Newbaum. She was smiling and handing out CDs with a full multimedia presentation of her vision for the school. Give a kid a computer and a CD burner and suddenly she's Bill Gates. Or Oprah. I'd be lucky to have an abacus.

But it wasn't Katia I was worried about. It was Stevie. I knew he wasn't done slinging his mud, and I needed a counterstrategy, something so brilliant he would fold like a house of cards.

I huddled Flora, Lloyd, Eraserhead, and Reese together like a football quarterback going over the final play of the big game.

"I've been thinking," Reese said.

Everyone burst out laughing.

"No, really. I have."

"Stop eating Mom's cookies," I suggested. "They're giving you delusions of grandeur."

"Eat them?" Reese was shocked. "No way! I use 'em to nail kids long-range."

"I know," Lloyd moaned and rubbed the back of his head.

"I think we should get some dirt on Stevie," Reese suggested. "Something to make him think twice about messing with us."

"You're on it, Reese," I said, assigning the task. "Lloyd. Flora. You're on poster duty. I did a study of the high-traffic areas for maximum poster saturation. Soda machine. Bathrooms —"

"You want us to hang posters in the bathrooms?" Flora asked.

"In the bathrooms, in the stalls, and especially near the mirrors. And hang posters by that hole in the fence the kids sneak through during lunch," I continued. "And in the arcade across the street."

"What about the library?" Flora asked. "Should we hang posters at the library?"

"That'd just be a waste of paper and tape," I replied. "Lloyd. Go to the office and get a mailing list of all the kids in school."

"They won't give me that," Lloyd whined.

"They will if you tell them you're working with the school fund-raising program to get donations from all the parents," I corrected. "We can start mailing flyers tomorrow."

I clapped my hands, and everyone raised from the huddle like warriors ready for battle — a battle of strategy, a battle of willpower, a battle of wits.

Well, except for Reese on that last one.

CHAPTER EiGHTEEN

As my friends scrambled off on their various assignments, I was left alone at the campaign table. That's when Katia walked up. She sat down on the other side of the table.

She wasn't a Krelboyne, which meant she still had a chance to grow up without major psychological scars. She had short black hair and was pretty tall.

The strange thing was, before I became a Krelboyne, I was in a few classes with her. She *seemed* normal. She hardly ever raised her hand to answer a question. She got as many C's as she did A's, she had friends, and no one made fun of her.

I have no idea why she's running for student government.

"Hey, Malcolm," she said in a tone that made me feel like she wanted something.

"Hey," I replied in a tone that said I knew she wanted something.

"You probably think I want something, huh?"

"What!" I faked shock. "Why would you ever say that?"

"I don't know. I've just been hearing the stuff you and Stevie have been saying about each other."

"Like what stuff?" I asked.

"You know. That you sleep with the light on."

I'm sorry I asked. But it could be worse, I guess. Stevie could be saying I wet my bed.

"And that you wet your bed," Katia continued.

When will I learn to quit while I'm ahead?

"I just wanted to ask," she continued. "It seems that things are getting a little . . . you know . . . dirty between you and Stevie. I mean, why are you guys doing all that?"

Why? Because just when I thought I hit rock bottom, the Krelboynes threw me a shovel. But is this really the Krelboynes' fault? I mean, sure they nominated me, but no one forced me and Stevie to start this feud.

"You know . . ." Katia started again. "What's all this got to do with being elected?"

"It's got nothing to do with the election," I finally replied. "It's got *everything* to do with winning. That's the difference. You want to be elected. I want to win."

"Wow. That's . . . you know . . . pretty intense."

Like I need this? Did I wake up this morning and say, "Please, life, send some creepy girl to question my motives?" So maybe Katia wasn't creepy, but I had a campaign to run. I didn't have time to chitchat with someone who I knew wouldn't vote for me.

That was like talking to Reese about his favorite book: Nothing but a waste of time.

Katia stood and looked at me. So far, she'd been

playing fair, always talking about things that would "improve" the school rather than slinging mud and making wild promises like me and Stevie.

Like *that'd* ever get her elected.

And there we were, just staring at each other like she was waiting for me to say something profound. Truth? I was looking over her shoulder at Stevie. He was surrounded by students, pointing at me and making everyone laugh.

I was losing valuable insult ground. I *had* to get rid of Katia. But how? How?

"Here," I said pulling another cookie from the shoe-box. "It's on me."

CHAPTER NiNETEEN

■ was still standing in the quad an hour later, drowning in a dark sea of handshakes and promises. Pushing the smiles, rubbing the elbows, browning the nose.

"I promise to only sell food in the cafeteria we can recognize. I promise the janitors will clean the gum from under all the tables at least once a year. I promise to play Dead Trout over the intercom during homeroom." I dealt out the promises like I was sitting at a card table. The kids ate it up.

"What about the exchange students?" Sven Ingerstromski asked. "What can you do to help them fit in better?"

"Exchange students?" I responded. "You mean the Geographically Shifted Pupils?"

"Geographically Shifted . . . ?" Sven said, nodding. "I like the sound of that."

"He's . . . good," Stevie hissed to Clyde. "Quick . . . we need . . . to . . . counter."

"A vote for Stevie is a vote for Stevie," Clyde chirped loudly from behind their table.

"That . . . wasn't . . . exactly . . . what I . . . had in . . . mind." Stevie shook his head at Clyde.

"Not snappy enough?" Clyde replied.

"I . . . promise . . . to . . . open a . . . second hole . . . in the . . . fence," Stevie called out to the gathered students.

"I'll tear down the fence!" I countered.

"Arcade . . . in the . . . cafeteria."

"With free games!"

Stevie leered at me.

"Free Internet access," I threw out.

"With . . . no . . . Parental . . . Lockout!"

A gasp of anticipation swept through the crowd.

"A . . . vote for . . . Malcolm is . . . a . . . vote for . . . an . . . ape," Stevie offered.

"Ape?! What do you mean calling me an ape, Owl Boy?" I stepped around the table.

"I . . . was . . . talking . . . about Reese," Stevie corrected. He pointed to Reese, who was outside the principal's office. Reese had pulled down one of Stevie's posters and was wrapping up some poor kid like a sausage.

"Sorry about the 'owl boy' comment," I offered.

"It's . . . just . . . what I . . . expected . . . from . . . you."

And what's that supposed to mean? He keeps acting like Reese is beating up the competition. Oh, wait a sec. Reese *is* beating up the competition.

"Don't . . . worry. I'm . . . starting . . . my . . . 'half-Krelboyne . . . half-normal'. . . campaign."

Is he talking about me? Stevie's making it sound like I'm a lab experiment gone wrong. Body of a boy, head of a Krelboyne! Don't vote for the freak monster with the ape brother!

"Oh yeah?" I shot back in anger. "Well, whoooo you gonna vote for, Owl Boy?"

After, like, an hour of leering, the bell rang. Stevie and Clyde spun around and left.

Like, I should feel bad? He was the one who started all the low blows. He was the one who started the name-calling. I'm just playing his game and I'm playing to win.

So why do I feel so rotten?

"Say thank you, Reese," a voice behind me said.

"The only time I'll say that is when you move out of the house." I turned — I knew it was Reese.

"Then I guess you won't want to see this." Reese took a manila folder — the kind that spies always use in movies — and dangled it in front of my face. "Ever hear of a 'permanent record'?" he taunted.

A permanent record? No way! Those don't really exist! It *had* to just be something teachers use to scare kids, like the boogeyman and college.

"You got Stevie's permanent record?"

"No way. Those things don't really exist," Reese responded and handed me the folder. "This is better."

I tore open the folder faster than Dewey tears apart his Christmas presents. What waited inside was better than any fat man in a red-and-white suit.

It was victory. My victory.

"Oh my gosh! I don't believe it," I beamed as I saw the photo. Stevie was dressed up as "Super Stevie." Red spandex, blue cape, and two large yellow "S's" emblazoned across his chest. I looked at the date on the back — July? That means it *wasn't* Halloween.

If this photo got out, his campaign would be ruined faster than Mom's Thanksgiving dinner.

"Where did you get this?" I asked, stunned.

"Never question a source," Reese replied. "But check out the cardboard flames he glued to the side of his chair. You could wreck him for life," Reese added with glee. I don't think I've ever seen Reese that happy. Not since the time Dewey's tongue got stuck to the inside of the freezer.

Then it hit me. Something that made Reese so happy just couldn't be right.

Monologue

Welcome to politics. In case you haven't figured it out yet, politics isn't about the best person winning, it's about the person with the best dirt winning.

What's up with that?

So now I've got this total evidence that would make me President for sure, but I don't know what to do. I know it's not the right thing to use Stevie's photo, but is it really the wrong thing? He started the name-calling and dirty tricks.

Okay, maybe Reese started the dirty tricks, but there's a big difference between me telling Reese to do stuff and just hoping he'll do stuff. That doesn't even make me an accomplice, right?

I know I need to defeat my opponent and win this election, but all this mud-slinging is really starting to bother me. And this photo just might make things worse. What if Stevie has secret dirt on me? I go ballistic, he'll go ballistic back.

This is too much pressure for a kid. I should only be worried about when the video rental has to be back at Blockbuster.

But drastic times call for drastic measures. I'm asking my family for help. Again.

If you're counting? That's twice in one week. What's my life coming to?

CHAPTER TWENTY

"And then he called me 'half-breed' and I called him 'Owl Boy' and then —"

"Owl Boy?"

"Yeah, 'cause of his glasses. And then after I said that, he left and Reese came running up with this picture of Super Stevie and he —"

"Super Stevie?"

"Yeah. He has all the powers of racing flames —"

"Oop! Commercials are over. Your time's up for the next eleven-and-one-half-minutes, son," Dad said and turned back to the TV.

I've been conflicted all day. I could use the photo to humiliate Stevie and end his campaign, but is that really the right thing to do? I thought my dad could give me some advice, but I've been trying to squeeze the whole story during commercial breaks on TV. And every time I get started, the commercials end and my dad starts watching *The Dukes of Hazzard* again. So now I have to wait until —

"Commercial! Go!" Dad quickly exhaled as if he were starting a race.

"So Reese came running up with Stevie's photo —"

"Why would Reese do that?" Dad questioned.

"Because Stevie and I are in a fight."

"Why?"

"Because he called me 'half-breed' and I called him 'Owl Boy' and then —"

"Owl Boy?"

"Yeah, 'cause of his gla — oh, never mind," I sighed and finally gave up. Sometimes talking to my dad is exactly like talking to a dad.

I slumped and shuffled out of the room.

"You still have forty-five seconds until Boss Hogg and the Dukes come back!" Dad called out.

Like a lost dog looking for its master, I wandered around the house until I finally found Mom. She was neck-deep in a bubble bath. Mom mixed with bubbles usually means "Go away Malcolm," but I knew once she heard my problems, it'd be different. This isn't just my usual whining. This is my usual whining with morals at stake. Or something.

"Go away, Malcolm," she said before I even knocked on the door.

How does she do that? I didn't even touch the door-knob and her Mom Radar was already signaling "Warning! Incoming child!"

"But, Mom!" I whined and opened the door anyway. "This is important!"

"And my private time isn't?"

If she wanted private time, why'd she have kids?

"And if you're thinking, 'If she'd wanted private time, why'd she have kids?'" Mom shot at me, "it's because there wasn't enough suffering in my life!"

There is no way she could know what I'm thinking unless she can read my mind — which is like so totally a mom thing to learn.

"But —"

"The only butt I want to see, Mister, is yours walking back out that door."

"It's just one question and it's important," I implored.

"Is anything burning?" Mom asked.

"No."

"Anyone choking?"

"No."

"Then it can wait," Mom said and slid deeper into the bubbles.

Okay. So that didn't go as well as I hoped. Isn't this some form of child neglect? I mean, shouldn't my needs come first? Always?

I think so, anyway.

I only had one option left. I never thought I would sink to such a low point in my life that I'd have to resort to such desperate measures. Who am I kidding? My whole life is nothing but sinking low and desperate measures.

" . . . and now I've got this photo. If I use it, I'll win the election, but Stevie will be ruined. I don't know what to do."

The room was eerily silent. It was one of those creepy silences that makes you wonder if the other person is even awake.

"I think you should blame it on Mr. Fiddles."

"Who's Mr. Fiddles?" I asked.

"He's the invisible man who breaks things in the house," Dewey said, pointing to a model airplane of mine that was broken.

"Dewey! You broke my model?" I shouted.

"No, I didn't," Dewey quickly defended. "Mr. *Fiddles* did."

It's so easy for little kids. Invisible people breaking things. Creatures under the bed losing stuff. When was the last time I could sit in class and say, "My invisible friend stole my homework"? Okay, when was the last time I tried that and it worked?

So nobody's telling me what I should do, so now I totally have to solve my problem myself. Does that stink or what? I'm just as confused as I was before, except now I know that invisible men are breaking my things.

I wish I were invisible sometimes. That would be so cool. I could get into movies and concerts and amusement parks for free. I could always escape Reese or the Krelboynes.

But the best thing would be to hear people say, "Where's Malcolm?" Because when people say that, it means

they can't find me, and if they can't
find me, it probably means I'm happy.
Invisible and happy.
I'm really starting to hate Mr. Fiddles.

CHAPTER TWENTY-ONE

First thing Monday, the mass of students marched slowly into the auditorium. They knew what was coming: an hour of speeches. No, not just speeches, but the worst kind of speeches: student speeches. Sure, it was better than sitting in class *learning*. But then, what isn't? Learning is like vegetables. Sure, it's good for you, but where's the chocolate?

Think about it.

Me, Stevie, the Milsons, Katia, and the rest of the candidates sat in a row on the stage. Before us was a sea of voters with gum, pudding cups, and Discmans. Like they care about *anything* we have to say. And now that I think about it? I really don't care much about what we have to say either.

All I cared about was the manila folder in my hand.

Dewey hadn't been much help. He was a much better listener than I ever thought, but in the end, he was more concerned with getting Tootsie Rolls than helping me solve my problem. And the whole Mr. Fiddles thing just started to get weird.

The candidates for Treasurer spoke first. Yeah, Treasurer. What's up with that? Does each grade really need a student Treasurer? I guess someone has to decide how to spend the loose change from the annual bake sale.

"And I promise the money from the annual bake sale will go to buy chocolate sprinkles for the cupcakes at next year's annual bake sale," the treasurer candidate said.

See?

After he was done, the candidate returned to his chair amid a small spattering of claps, mostly from the teachers. The students would have to be awake to clap.

Next came the candidates for Vice President. Vice President? Even in real life Vice President is a loser job. So it must be a mega-loser job in a school election. Like, if the President is expelled, the VP gets to take over? *That's* a position I want. It's like being assistant librarian.

The best part is? Two girls running for Vice President are sisters. And not just sisters; twins. The Bernabe twins. They both think this is the launching point to a career in movies. Like talent scouts go to school assemblies looking for the next star?

"And the reason you shouldn't vote for my sister," Bernabe twin number one said into the microphone, "is because *she* can't act."

"Well, at least I don't sleep with a Mrs. Fiddles doll!" Bernabe twin number two stood from her chair and shouted.

"The therapist made you promise not to tell!" twin number one cried.

"Girls! Girls!" the principal said, rushing to the podium. "Let's stick with the issues."

"These *are* the issues!" the twins both spat back in unison.

The sad part is? That was the high point of the day.

While the future Academy Award–winning Bernabe twins argued, I leaned over to Stevie. "There's something you should know," I said in a whisper.

"Unless . . . you're . . . dropping . . . out . . . I'm not . . . interested," Stevie replied.

"I'm not dropping out, but I think you'll still be interested."

I pulled out the manila folder from under my shirt and held it out to Stevie.

"Is . . . that . . . what . . . I think . . . it is?" Stevie asked, a slight quiver in his voice.

"No. Those don't exist."

Stevie gave a sigh of relief.

"But it is a photo of the first appearance of . . . Super Stevie."

Stevie's eyes widened as I revealed the photo.

"I . . . told . . . my mom . . . this . . . would . . . come back . . . to . . . haunt me," Stevie said in dismay. "Flames. What . . . was . . . I . . . thinking?"

"Don't make me use this, Stevie," I said, trying not to sound like I was threatening him.

"Are . . . you . . . threaten . . . ing . . . me?"

So much for that.

"I'm just saying that it won't matter how many

school days or tax cuts you promise. You know what this will do."

He was on the brink of dropping out, I could tell. Then I'd win. This whole stupid election would be over and I could focus on getting those Dead Trout concert tickets. So it was a little sketchy. Life is unfair, and so is politics.

Stevie finally looked up at me again. He was about to say it: "I quit." "You win." "It's all yours." It didn't really matter. Victory was mine!

Stevie looked at me with his big eyes. "Do . . . what you . . . want," was all he said before he rolled away.

CHAPTER TWENTY-TWO

Why didn't he just drop out? No. He couldn't do that and make my life easy. Instead, he makes *me* decide what to do. I *hate* that.

I don't know if I should make a speech or just crawl under a rock. Since there was no rock, I slowly made my way to the podium. Trust me, it was a *long* walk.

"Malcolm for President!" a red-haired girl called out.

The crowd started to cheer and chant, "Malcolm for President! Malcolm for President! Malcolm for President!" over and over. I stood at the podium and looked out over the students and teachers. In the back of the auditorium, I saw Reese holding some kid in a headlock, forcing him to chant "Malcolm for President!" with the others.

It was Clyde, Stevie's campaign manager.

Where's Mr. Fiddles when you really need him? Heck, I couldn't blame this on Mr. Fiddles. This was all my fault. I didn't mean for things to get out of hand. Honest.

My head hurt.

I wanted to win, but I didn't want to actually *be* President, which must mean that I didn't want to win, but I wanted to beat Stevie, which meant I'd be President. And the only reason I wanted to beat Stevie was because he started saying all that crud about me, which he only did because he was mad when I told him I didn't want to be President.

My head hurt even more.

"Thank you," I began, hushing the crowd.

The manila folder was in my right hand, and I could barely hold it. It was only one photo, but it felt like it weighed a ton.

"Look, I just wanted to tell you I can't give you a two-hour lunch or whatever other crazy promises I made."

"What about paid vacations for the students?" some girl yelled out. "You promised that, too."

"I can't do that, either."

The girl pulled her "MALCOLM IS MAGIC LIKE SANTA" button from her sweater and threw it on the ground.

"But what I can promise is that if you vote for me, I'll do my best to be your class President. I guess that means honesty and effort and whatever stuff class Presidents do. Except for the meetings, I don't even *know* what class Presidents do. Is that sad, or what?"

Some students in the audience looked at each other, confused.

"And the reason I don't know is because I didn't want to run for President. Because, like, who cares, y'know? But then suddenly, nothing was more important to me than winning. I still really don't care about this whole President thing, it's just that I didn't want to lose. But sometimes when we fight for what we think we want, we forget what's really important.

"But, you know, vote for me and I'll do my best. That's all. My best."

And that was it. As I walked back to my seat, the red-haired girl yelled out, "You stink!" but that was it.

I walked over to Stevie and held my hand out.

"May the best man win?" I asked.

"You . . . bet," Stevie said excitedly, gripping my hand as if he was clinging to a life preserver. After a moment, he let go, smiled at me, and then wheeled to the microphone for his speech.

Cool. Stevie and I are friends again. The competition is over. Now we don't have to worry about who's going to win and who's going to lose. No more lies and crazy promises.

"Elect . . . me . . . and I . . . promise to . . . abolish homework." Stevie hurriedly wheezed into the microphone.

And the crowd went wild.

Okay. So I feel totally better now. I know I did the right thing, and it feels good to be able to say that. While everyone voted, I gave Stevie the "Super Stevie" evidence and he gave me some photos he made on the computer. Me wearing a dress!

"Just in . . . case," he said.

Twisted. I think that's why I like Stevie so much.

So then we voted and when I'm standing in the booth, I just suddenly get this feeling that the right thing to do is to vote for Stevie. But get this: When I tell him, he says "Thanks," then rolls away.

"Did you vote for me?" I call out.

"You'll . . . never . . . know."

Totally twisted.

CHAPTER TWENTY-THREE

The following Friday night, Reese and I sat in the living room watching TV. We really didn't care what we were watching as long as it was TV. Like my mom's bubble baths and Dad's quadraphonic records, this is our time. Time to chill and let the brain turn to Jell-O. Sure, TV rots your mind. I wouldn't have it any other way.

"Well, I can see by the fact that both of you are watching TV that the Great Frame Game was a failure," Francis said, coming in the front door. "You two sitting on the couch watching TV like two cozy lovebirds wasn't really the level of chaos I was hoping to create."

In his heart, Francis had hoped to walk into a home on the brink of crisis: Mom and Dad at the end of their ropes; Reese and I locked in separate rooms; Dewey on the loose. Then Francis could swoop in and save the day — and come home for good.

Instead all he got was two exhausted brothers eating stale cereal from the box and watching *Universal Slambots 2001*.

"If you'd let us light things on fire, we wouldn't have all this peace!" Reese defended.

"I wanted trouble, dude. Not funerals."

"Look, Francis, we both know we let you down and it's not your fault," I explained. "We could have tried harder."

"I obviously need to spend more time teaching you two the ways of guerrilla warfare and household destabilization. Your failures are my fault, young master Malcolm," Francis said. "It's a poor carpenter who blames his tools."

Francis's wisdom is the coolest.

"What does cutting wood have to do with this?" Reese blurted out.

"Never mind," Francis said and plopped on the couch next to me. "I still have to take someone to see Dead Trout or I can't go. The question is: Which one of you little future delinquents should I choose?"

"I'll do your chores for a month!" Reese quickly said, jumping up from the couch.

"I don't have any chores," Francis returned.

"I'll hide any mail you don't want Mom and Dad to see," I offered.

"You already do," Francis pointed out.

This is tough. It's like getting a birthday present for the kid who has everything. But in the end, there's always one thing that'll win the day . . .

"Eight dollars!" I shouted.

"Ten!" Reese countered.

"Fifteen!"

"Fifteen-fifty!"

"Fifteen-seventy!"

"Fifteen-seventy-two!"

"Stop! Stop!" Francis yelled. "Fifteen dollars won't even buy me a hot dog at the concert. There aren't enough zeros in both of your bank accounts to bribe a ticket from me."

Reese and I flopped back onto the couch. Desperation time. If bribery and flattery won't work, I'm all out of ideas.

"Seems we'll have to let George settle this one," Francis said, reaching into his pocket. He pulled out a quarter and held it before Reese and me.

"What are we supposed to do with that?" Reese asked.

"Call heads or tails, doofus," I responded, rolling my eyes.

"And then what?"

If you can't eat it, punch it, or break it, Reese is at a total loss.

Francis took the coin and laid it on his thumb. In mere seconds one of us would be staying home and the other would be on his way to the mosh pit with Francis, pounding bodies to the awesome sounds of Dead Trout.

"Heads!" I called and Francis flipped the coin.

Francis caught the quarter in midair and clenched it in his right hand. In a quick motion, he slapped it down atop his left hand and peeked at the results.

"We have a winner!" he announced, then grinned. He waited for seconds, then minutes. He was going to make us suffer, and there was nothing we could do about it.

"Who is it?" Reese implored. "Who won?"

"Dewey," Francis said with a smile.

"Dewey!" Reese and I exploded back in unison.

"But Mom said you had to take one of us!"

"No. Mom said I had to take one of my *brothers*," Francis corrected. "And since neither of you won the Great Frame Game, I have to go with the backup candidate."

"I'm ready to go to the zoo," Dewey said to Francis as he entered the room.

"Concert, Dewey. You mean concert," Francis responded.

"The animals are going to sing?" Dewey eagerly asked.

"But . . . but . . . but . . ." I stammered. If I was going to save the day, I'd better come up with something better than stammering conjunctions. "You said!"

Oh, yeah. *That's* a winner.

"Dude," Francis began, "you guys failed in the Great Frame Game. What kind of message would I be sending if I rewarded failure?"

"What about the carpenter and his tools?" I implored.

"Pfff. That's just some crud I heard in a movie."

Dewey? Beaten by the creator of Q-Tip Town? Next thing you know, someone's going to tell me I lost the election to Katia.

Oh, by the way, I did lose the election to Katia. When all the votes were counted, I lost. When they were recounted, I lost again. And when they were recounted again, I still lost. It's bad enough to lose an election. It's worse to keep losing it. Just ask Al Gore.

Stevie didn't win, either. It turns out the Krelboynes voted right down the middle – exactly half for me and the other half for Stevie. Nobody else in our grade voted for us, so we tied for last place.

The Milson twins dropped out of the race. They got some new games for their Playstation and lost interest in student government. In fact, they lost interest in everything except trying to outscore each other in Terminator's Super-Baseball 9000.

But I wasn't the biggest loser. That would be Francis.

When Mom found out he decided to take Dewey to the concert, her eyes bugged out and she turned, like, purple. "You thought you'd take a child to a heavy metal concert? Are you insane?"

For punishment? She actually made Francis take him to the zoo — at the same exact time of the concert.

So if you do the math, you'd think that left both tickets unused. But since you have to add my family to the equation, you could figure how it really turned out.

Now _my_ parents are like huge Dead Trout fans. That's all I needed.

I'm just glad it's all over. Stevie and I are friends again. Reese isn't trying to frame me. And Mom's not making any more cookies. Everything is back to normal.

Yeah, like that's gonna last.